# Her Teeth, Like Waves

By

Nikki R. Leigh

This book is a work of fiction. Names, characters, places, and incidents are the product of the author's imagination or are used fictitiously. Any resemblance to actual events, locales, or persons, living or dead, is coincidental.

*Her Teeth, Like Waves*. Copyright © 2022 by Nikki R. Leigh

First Edition

Cover copyright and design © 2023 by Matt Wildasin.

Published by Spooky House Press, LLC.
East Islip, NY, 11730, USA
www.spookyhousepress.com

All rights reserved. No part of this book may be reproduced, stored
in a retrieval system, or transmitted in any form or by any means, including but not limited to electronic, electrostatic, magnetic, tape, mechanical, photocopying, recording, or otherwise without permission from the author.

ISBN: 978-1-959946-12-0 (Paperback)

ISBN: 978-1-959946-13-7 (eBook)

Printed in the United States of America

# Praise for
# *Her Teeth, Like Waves*

"Nikki R. Leigh writes about the meanest, most lethal waters this side of Peter Benchley. Like the unfathomable predator of this compelling narrative, her prose is made of teeth, and she does use them to bite. *Her Teeth, Like Waves* is the best kind of reading for a day on the beach. Just don't throw anything into the waves, and if you do, certainly do not go into the water after it."

- Douglas Ford, author of *Little Lugosi (A Love Story)* and the best-selling *The Beasts of Vissaria County*

"Unexplored cave systems deep under the ocean should stay that way, but where would be the fun in that? Nikki Leigh reaches into the depths of our lizard brains to bring our worst fears to life, confirming what I've always suspected: water is cruel, unknowable, and full of teeth. A swift and unsettling read, sure to create new phobias."

- Laurel Hightower, author of *Crossroads* and *Below*

*This book is dedicated to my forever gal.*
*I'd go anywhere you want to take me.*

# Table of Contents

Part One. Unearthed ................................................................. 1

Part Two. Awakening .............................................................. 13

Part Three. Destabilize ............................................................ 35

Part Four. Churn ..................................................................... 57

Part Five. Swallow .................................................................. 71

Epilogue. Regurgitate .............................................................. 91

*The sea! The sea!*

*Tumbling waves that beat your chest.*

*The sea! The sea!*

*Calls you close. Her lips are cleft.*

*The sea! The sea!*

*White teeth rage, her sands a nest.*

*The sea! The sea!*

*Takes it all. Nothing left.*

- Children's song from the coast of the Pacific

*The sea! The sea!*

*Tumbling waves that beat your chest.*

*The sea! The sea!*

*Calls you close. Her lips are cleft.*

*The sea! The sea!*

*White teeth rage, her sands a nest.*

*The sea! The sea!*

*Takes it all. Nothing left.*

                    - Children's song from the coast of the Pacific

# Part One.
# Unearthed

Mitch knew he was playing in a sandbox that he wasn't invited to.

A big, never-ending, serpentine dune of sand under fifty meters of crystal blue water.

The sandbox he was looking for—a winding set of caves carved by God knows what into the walls of rock submerged in the sea—was only a short dive away. And as the top of his head plunged under the water and the gentle embrace of the ocean enveloped him, Mitch was ready to go the distance.

Down he went, his gear like a second set of skin for his body. The muffled sounds of his fellow divers following his direction surrounded him one after another until five bodies were gliding through the water towards the dark depths.

The mouth of the cave beckoned, its pull so strong a current that Mitch wondered if it could be fought against. The thumping in his chest reminded him that this is what he wanted.

That there would be no struggle because the current would take him where he desired to go. Mitch smiled, certain that he was feeling the same excitement his parents did when they found such sights to photograph.

The last rays of sun kissed the lips of the dark caves, and he hesitated at the opening of the shadowed hole. As he hovered in the water, contemplating his choice to enter the sure to be dangerous terrain, a glint of gold caught his eye. The chain around his wrist, holding his father's wedding band, floated in front of him. One of the only things pulled from the wreckage of his parents' plane crash. The end of their journey.

The gold band glimmered, pulled forward by the current, and pointed towards the caves. The end of their journey. The beginning of his own.

This had to be the place. *Had to*. The years of planning and searching, of trading bits of himself for parts of the map. Piecing together tragedies of the coast until he uncovered the coordinates of his destination.

Into the cave. As he crossed the threshold, the light of

## Part One. Unearthed

the shining sun was diminished by the thick gray and brown walls, and Mitch thought of his sister. How she shunned her sense of wonder for the deep to a place where she could smother the grief in her heart at their parents' death. He wished she could embrace the call of the ocean instead and let the waves whisper her further along to find the darkest places and illuminate them.

Just like him. Just like this trip.

In fact, he could almost hear the call now. The sound of a woman weeping, distant on his ears. Another mystery of the deep. He wondered if only he could hear the sounds, like a set of sonar designed solely for him. He looked around to his fellow divers, his friends who wanted adventure as much as he. They looked back to him for direction, to lead them to their glory. The humming of the ocean pulled him deeper.

Mitch pushed his thoughts away, taking in the vastness of the winding caves. The stories had promised treasure. Mitch didn't know if that meant gold or a new discovery. He didn't really care. The only stake he planned to claim was to be the one to make it there and back, a story of his own. He collected memories like they were precious diamonds, after all.

Mitch almost felt bad, pulling the group below when he couldn't promise them gold. But he had to do this. Had to make it to the caves and see it through. The tales of the system haunted him, as heavy in his mind as the ghosts of his parents in his heart. *Legacy, adventure, legends.*

Around him, his fellow divers, cameras mounted to their goggles, signaled the directions they would go. The plan was to traverse five minutes in one direction, then return to the mouth of the cave to devise a new route. The map he had drawn ended here, only given coordinates to the cave system itself, the rest seemingly unexplored.

Mitch went straight ahead, his friends at his back, flippers propelling him further into the system. His heart pounded in anticipation of what he would find. So far, he'd seen no sea creatures or the green of plant life. Just rock and sand.

So different from his other trips into the crevices of the ocean. He often found that the deeper he went, the brighter things were. Colors, chirps of sound, the shine of the sun above like thin rays of glass penetrating the veneer of the blue.

But here, the caves just grew darker and darker as he sliced through the tunnel. He felt vaguely afraid, but Mitch swallowed it down into a tightening chest. His determination to explore and find something worthwhile pulsated through his body and out his fingertips. Water filtered through his outstretched hands, grasping at nothing, but reaching for more.

Mitch began to feel the familiar tug of changing pressure in his chest as he swam. The weight of depths began to take its toll; his lungs felt like the walls of the cave, closing in on itself. He fought through the panic, forward, forward, forward the only direction he'd let his mind obey.

The darkness muddied his thoughts. The silence of the ocean overwhelming, words bubbling up and down and across his mind.

But then… humming. Then weeping. A sound that cut through the vastness of the deep to bring direction to his mind. Clarity.

The humming grew louder. A whisper of sadness

became a crescendo of despair. A singsong of sobs like a compass in the dark.

*Push*, Mitch thought to himself. *Deeper*. Repeating the words in his head, he propelled himself further still. He didn't think about how the five minutes had likely passed, that his friends had hopefully reconvened in the cave opening. He didn't think about how every kick of his feet made him a little more lost.

He didn't think, but he sure did feel. Pressure like a one-ton weight dragged him through the caves. A sharp *cracking* sound indicated that his lamplight had broken. Only darkness now, but Mitch didn't need to see anymore.

The magnetic pull of the caves wound him through her intestines, the walls getting narrower until suddenly, Mitch could move only an inch further at a time. The sides squeezed his ribs and ripped his oxygen tank from his back. Did he need to breathe? He gulped one last lungful of air from his diving apparatus before the tank clunked to the sandy floor. His breathing tube ripped from his mouth, dancing like a headless

## Part One. Unearthed

snake to the depths below.

Forward, forward more, his arms stretched in front of him, Mitch finally found the treasure. A cul-de-sac of the cave's interior, a bulb of open space. His hands grasped open sea, even while his stomach dragged on the floor.

He choked on what little oxygen remained in his lungs. A blinding pearl of light suddenly illuminated the pitch dark. It pulsated and glowed, beckoning to him. The orb, its glassy bright exterior nestled in a tangle of cloth.

In the center of the opening, just out of reach from his fingertips, another small sphere appeared, maybe a half-inch in diameter, nestled in the sand before Mitch's eyes. His vision wavered as he began to suffocate, but he found the strength to reach with trembling fingertips, bolstered by the water's cushion.

One finger, just the barest tip of his gloved hand, so close. He just needed one more push. He dug into the sand, jerked himself forward with a burst of energy, the rock walls tearing at his sides, ripping skin from his hips. The cave wanted to keep him where he was, but Mitch didn't care. Didn't notice the way the cave groaned as he was released.

Air gone. Oxygen depleted. Water filled Mitch's sinuses and his throat. His eyes watered as the ocean entered his lungs. Tears meant nothing in the vastness of the sea. Another drop in her bucket.

Finally, his finger and the glowing glass orb met. The tiniest *tink* under what felt like miles of ocean, resonating throughout the caves. The force was just enough to unsettle the orb, to free it from its cloth and sand prison.

As Mitch, dying, sank to the gritty ground, the orb, rejuvenated, rose.

The last thing Mitch heard was the mounting sobs of the ocean, filling his ears with sorrowful rage.

Purposefully, the glass orb darted about the cave, calling forth what it desired. Its light pulsated like a firefly, awakening the world around it.

It gathered. It sang. It took its collection through the cave system, tracing Mitch's last movements.

## Part One. Unearthed

It—awoken, angry, hungry—found.

The divers had reconvened at the mouth of the cave, awaiting Mitch's directions back to their boat. They hovered near the entrance, checking tank levels, watches, fighting the urge to go where Mitch had been. Resisting the call back to the surface of the water, where oxygen wouldn't be a concern.

The divers didn't know what Mitch had wrested from the sand. Didn't know that it had already culled minions from the ocean floor. Discarded teeth. Fragments of broken rock. Offerings to the vast depths.

As the orb zipped towards the entrance of the cave, the first diver was consumed. Ripped to shreds in a violent whirlpool of red and teeth and bubbles. The divers couldn't scream.

Sand churned violently around the group of underwater cavers. They had no hope of seeing their hands in front of their faces. No way to check how many fingers remained, how many bloodied stumps they were left with.

Panic stripped the divers of their ability to think, so they kicked harder and harder, digging more sand up from below into a muddied cloud. They pressed their bodies as close to the side of the cave as they could, rocky abutments digging into their backs, hardly felt against the backdrop of pain from their missing limbs and chunks of skin displaced from their bodies.

A lone diver hovered in the middle of the cave, daring the creature to take him. He flapped his feet, screamed through his mouthpiece.

He was gone in a flash of teeth. A full body in the water one second, bits and pieces the next.

Through the chum of his body, the other divers gasped and winced, praying they could avoid the destruction by staying hidden against the walls.

The sand kicked up violently once again. The divers saw nothing. No body, no head, only a disconnected flash of white serrated triangles.

A circle of teeth, spinning like a garbage disposal, darted forward and began to eat. The sand rose again. Water rushed through the cave, a tsunami of brown, blue, and red.

# Part One. Unearthed

# Part Two.
# Awakening

"He hasn't checked in for four days now," Kat said. She was pacing back and forth across her tiny apartment, her kitten weaving through her legs in attempts to trip her towards the kitchen and her food.

Jules reached out to grab Kat's shoulders and stop the pacing. "He probably just broke his phone or something. You know that goon is always losing it in the water."

Kat continued her pacing, shaking free of her girlfriend's grip. She ran her hands nervously through her long blond hair. Her hazel eyes flickered with pain. She thought of all the other times her brother had called or emailed her, telling her about the latest girl he had a falling out with, the next trip he would take.

"He always calls. He finds a way."

"Your brother probably just met some girl and went bar hopping with her, having the time of his life. It *is* Spring Break after all."

"Spring Break, where the island is overflowing with people. You've seen *Piranha 3DD*. You know that's when things in the ocean like to eat."

"I highly doubt schools of prehistoric fish are eating your brother."

Kat stopped her pacing for a moment, trying to breathe. She didn't know why she was getting so worked up. Jules was right that her brother would sometimes go silent for a few days. Just never right before a long dive. He always checked in, doing the one thing he could to ease Kat's worries about the dangers of his hobby. And now, that feeling in her gut…she felt like something was wrong with her twin.

Kat had never really subscribed to the weird twin mumbo jumbo. That they could feel each other over long distances. That they lived parallel lives and had similar thoughts and personalities, and were all but attached at the hip just because they shared a shit-ton of genes. She'd always just written if off as one of those things she'd spend the rest of her life explaining to strangers when they inevitably asked her if she and Mitch

## Part Two. Awakening

were like that. Psychically linked.

But then, three days ago it hit her like a sledgehammer, deep in her chest. It felt like the wind was knocked from her, air exploding from her lungs, a pain in her stomach. Hit with a sharp, blunt object that didn't exist until she was doubled-over.

She felt shredded. The dishes had clattered from her hands, dropping hard onto the metal sink below. A shard had cut her hand. Jules had walked in to see her standing there, dripping blood from the wound over the sink, breathing shallowly.

She'd tried to reach Mitch since then, calling his phone, texting him, sending an email. No answer. The last she'd heard he was taking groups of divers on expeditions in the Channel Islands to check out underwater caves. He seemed more excited than usual. Rambling on about some unexplored system.

It wasn't like they'd never been to the Channel Islands before. They'd visited plenty as kids, a favorite destination of their parents. Kat knew it wasn't out of the question for him to be spending so much time there, but the persistent nagging in her stomach said otherwise. Bits and pieces of stories she'd heard about the Islands as kids invaded her memory. Tales of mysterious disappearances, deaths in the depths of the ocean and no sharks or other creatures to blame.

Kat chided herself for not saying something during Mitch's last phone call. But she knew she wouldn't have been able to convince him just how dangerous his journey could be, no matter what. She'd tried in the past when he planned to chart treacherous water, and all her suggestions would earn her was a cold shoulder and slow updates on his status. She'd learned to bite her tongue.

She didn't understand his fascination with the caves. She found them to be terrifying; the only thing worse than open water was being squeezed into a tight space while submerged. Though they'd both trained to dive, Kat planned on never getting in the water again.

For most of her life she shared her parents' love of the ocean, enjoyed the feeling of total submersion, the silence of the sea. Her mother was an underwater photographer, and her father ran a diving equipment company, so the family took trips to

## Part Two. Awakening

exotic locations nearly every summer.

She remembered their last trip, before the accident. The first time she'd seen the coral reefs outside of Australia. She remembered the colors, the life, the diversity of everything. She took it all in, her eyes jumping from creature to plant to shimmering ray of light beaming through the blue curtain. She wanted to know it all. Document it.

But as she got older and began studying the ocean in earnest, she became utterly terrified of the unknown. Dark waters held dark stories, undiscovered creatures, dangers in every kelp bed. The more she learned about the ocean, the more she learned just how *wrong* things in the ocean could go. That beyond the dangers of diving itself, there was almost too much unknown. That the metaphorical tides could change at any moment.

Kat could always recall one of her first negative encounters with the ocean, vicarious as it was, that sent her seven-year-old brain on the fritz. She could almost hear the way her parents talked in hushed tones one night, stifling tears. Her

Mother, phone to her ear, held a hand over her mouth as she quietly wept. The next day, Kat learned that her parents' oldest friend, a diving exhibitionist, had drowned. She'd taken trips with him before, always admiring the way he could knife through the water, point out little secrets of the sea. Kat remembered wondering how his death was possible, that every time she'd gone with him the open air was just overhead.

But their friend hadn't just been casually diving. He'd taken to exploring the deepest parts of the ocean he could find. Parts that were barely accessible without submarines. Kat could see the ways her parents were conflicted in how they explained his death—chiding him for taking risks too big. Commending him for finding new corners of the ocean to expose. Those memories summed up her own complex feeling towards her twin.

"Earth to Kat," Jules said, wrapping her arms around Kat. "Earth to my very worried looking girlfriend."

"Sorry I was just…"

"Spiraling? I could tell. I thought you might start actually spinning and drill a hole into the floor."

Kat sighed, fingering her bracelet around her wrist. "I'm just so worried about him."

"Why don't we just go?"

"To the islands? The Channel Islands?"

"Yeah, we can look for Mitch, and when we find him safe and sound, we can have a nice little vacation."

"You'd be okay with that? I don't think anything else will help me settle my mind."

"I'm totally okay with it. Impromptu vacations are the best. Flesh-eating piranhas and all."

Kat narrowed her eyes at Jules, who laughed at her concerned girlfriend.

"I promise I'm taking this seriously, Kat. I trust your gut about the twin stuff. I just want good energy out in the air. He'll be okay."

"I hope so. Let's get packed. Just a few hours of driving between us and a peace of mind. Thank you, Jules."

"Anything for you," Jules said. The two stood together,

foreheads touching. After a short time, they pulled apart, fighting their gravitational pull towards one another, like a wave to shore.

Later that night, after an hour of disorganized packing, Kat stared at the ceiling in their bedroom. Jules was lightly snoring next to her, and Kat found herself jealous of the ease with which she had fallen asleep. Kat was wide awake, unable to rest her troubled mind, imagining Mitch in all scenarios, likely and unlikely. Laughing and knocking back a drink at the bar. Bloodied in the mouth of shark. Staring off the bow of a ship, setting his sights on his destination, excitement crinkling his eyes. Floating face down in the chop of the waves.

The images were coming so fast and steadily that her senses kaleidoscoped, turning over and over to the point of nausea. No matter what she did, she couldn't get her mind to stop producing the series of horrifically juxtaposed images. She laid there, eyes on a bare ceiling, projecting images of catastrophe and glee, blood and smiles. She could almost smell the rot of his dead skin, could almost taste the booze and fruit,

## Part Two. Awakening

could almost feel her fingers prodding bloated and barnacled skin.

After a couple of hours of convincing herself that it had to stop (it didn't), and that she was doing the only thing she could by taking the trip (there had to be more to do), she finally closed her eyes. She willed her face to relax, feeling her forehead to unwrinkle, her mouth to grow slack.

Finally, she slept, hearing a faint humming deep in the recesses of her thoughts. A gentle lull that rose and fell like waves. She was sleeping, but a part of her had woken up.

#

The couple took the next day to drive up the coast of California. They committed to a solid three and half hours to drive to the dock on the coast, and another hour by boat to reach the islands. They'd packed a few belongings into suitcases in a haste and took to the road by early morning sun.

Kat's nerves ran rampant the whole drive, her feet tapping nervously on the floor of the car. At one point, she leaned her head against the cool glass of the passenger seat window and closed her eyes, willing time and distance to pass much faster than it was. The smooth grinding wheels on the road soon turned to buzzing in her head as she began to drift off.

Her thoughts were on her brother as she dozed, and as she fell into a state of half sleep as a memory pushed her further under. Ten years old, in the cabin of a boat, Mitch and Kat began to lace their life vests, preparing for a foray into the water while their parents explored the reefs nearby.

Kat remembered the twinkle in Mitch's eye—something daring, something kind of shitty—right before he tackled her to the floor. Kids doing kid things, wrestling, nothing out of the norm for the pair. Kat was never one to back down to Mitch's bursts of energy, and all too often their parents had to pry one off the other before they busted their heads open on the coffee table or fireplace or sidewalk curb.

But this time, Kat remembered feeling something for the first time. She'd always been able to wiggle out of her brother's grasp, but on this occasion, Mitch pushed her, face first into the floor, and sat on her. Squarely above her shoulder blades, he

## Part Two. Awakening

perched. Taunting her, telling her he was stronger than her.

In her liminal state, Kat, with the grounding sensation of her face against the hard glass of the car window, could still feel the pressure mounting on her chest. Her face scrunched in torment, feeling the weight of her brother on her back, her arms pinned at her sides by his spindly legs. She couldn't push off the ground, couldn't take a proper breath. She was trapped, vulnerable.

And Mitch didn't care.

It was one of the only times Kat remembered a cruelness to her brother. A change happening within him as he exerted his power over her. With a voice full of ire, Mitch leaned down and whispered to his squirming sister.

"Mom says that when you dive too deep, your body gets crushed."

"Get off me, Mitch!" Kat yelled.

"You think it feels like this?" he asked, his voice losing its edge.

Though at the time Kat felt panicked, felt her lungs

struggle against her own flesh and blood, in her dreamlike state, she finally saw it for what it was.

Fear. Her brother, usually so ready to embrace the waves and ocean for all it was worth, was for the first time grappling with what could go wrong. Kat had already lived in that space for a couple of years, ever since her parents' friend died when she was seven.

But it had taken longer for Mitch, always seeing the ocean as a playground to explore rather than what it was—an immense beast that could take all it wanted. The ocean would never drown, would never die of starvation. The ocean, Kat knew, was a glutton for life, making everything else its own.

Kat hadn't revisited this particular memory for at least a decade, but now she wondered what had made things finally click into place for Mitch. What had caused him to force his fear on her that day.

He wasn't a bad guy, her brother. But in that moment, he had terrified her. Though he had eventually dismounted her back, had put his hand behind his head as he stood, looking onto her crying, gasping form, something had broken between them.

He'd offered an apology, rubbed the back of his head, staring at his feet.

She told him to screw off, eyes clouded with tears. Stormed off like an angry little tempest, too afraid to even tell Mom and Dad.

"You okay?"

Jules' voice pulled her from her half slumber, her partner's hand caressing her thigh.

"Just a bad dream. Bad memory."

Jules looked at her briefly before turning her attention back to the road.

"You're drooling."

And so she was.

#

Kat spent the entire hour-long boat ride looking out to the sea, wondering what was lying below the depths of the brackish water. The wind blew her hair around wildly, dancing like streamers in front of her face, falling into her mouth. She puckered her lips and puffed her hair from her face. The air tasted of salt.

She tried to give space to the voice in her head that said she was overreacting, that the quick decision road trip was unnecessary and that her brother was fine. But she also kept hearing an echo, a scream in a void where she normally felt a fullness, the connection that brought her to her twin. That hole, the missing part of her, beat out the voice in her head. She felt lucky to have Jules at her side.

The boat engine continued to whir, the water bubbled in waves behind them, carving railroad tracks into the ocean's surface. She only hoped it was bringing her closer to her brother.

After a quiet hour on the boat, Kat and Jules down a rickety ramp to the dock, fingers interlocked, holding tight. Kat knew that Jules could sense how nervous she was and chose to let her think through her thoughts, knowing that sometimes she just needed to work through the swirling anxiety.

The pair walked along the docks, looking out for the sign for the small hotel they'd booked, something cheap for a few days while Kat tried to locate her brother. Jules was hoping for a nice bit of vacation time, that everything would be just fine. But the closer they got to the island, the more her hope fell, like an anchor to the ocean floor, dragging her mood down into the dark.

At the hotel, they checked in and dropped off their lightly packed luggage. The day was still young, so they planned to hit the local bar by the diving expedition scene. They wanted to put some feelers out for Mitch, see where he had recently booked an expedition.

They passed a gaggle of children, jump-roping and singing. Kat could barely make out the words. Something about the sea and her waves and taking. Whatever it was, Kat was taken aback that a) kids still jump-roped and sang, something she'd previously believed only happened in the movies; and b) that songs kids sang never stopped being ridiculously dark and depressing. Kat and Jules exchanged a look before laughing nervously.

The two continued their walk to the bar, a good half mile

away. Kat tried to take in the beauty of their travels.

"It's just like I remember it," she said to Jules. "My parents took us here a lot as kids. Every summer this was our first destination. Dad always wanted to check in on what people were using locally to dive. Mom wanted to dive. She took some of her most beautiful photographs here."

Kat grew quiet. Jules rubbed her fingers over Kat's knuckles.

"I always loved the ones you have in the apartment. They're so bright. So much life," Jules said.

Kat nodded. "I feel lucky we were able to hold onto those after the accident. A lot of her photos were whisked away when she died. Mitch and I were too young to know how to properly fight for them. He was all I had after Mom and Dad were killed."

Jules let the silence grow. She knew it was hard for Kat to talk about her family, since her parents were killed in a private plane crash when Kat and Mitch were sixteen years old. Jules was thankful the twins grew closer rather than being driven apart by the tragedy. Even though now, at twenty-eight, Mitch lived

## Part Two. Awakening

most of his time on the islands and Kat was far inland with Jules, the two kept in constant contact with one another.

The pair trekked on, nearing the bar. The more that Kat took in the island, the more the stories she'd heard as a kid flooded into her mind. She wouldn't let them stop her now though, not after coming this far. Kat pushed the tales of carnage back down, swallowing her fear.

The sounds of clinking glass and laughter rose as they stepped closer. Hands still held together, the two entered the bar, scanning for any sign of Mitch, hoping to see his shaggy blonde head of hair bobbing as he knocked back a beer.

Kat deflated at Jules' side. Not a single blonde head to be seen. Mitch wasn't there. The two figured it wouldn't be that easy, so they walked up to the bar and sat on the rickety stools. The day had been long already, so they decided to grab a couple of pints and ask around the bar, which was occupied by more than a few haggard looking fishermen and seafarers.

Kat nursed a pint in front of her, eyes on the white froth at the rim of the glass, starkly contrasted against the gold of her beer. An older woman sidled up next to her, a half full beer stein in her hand.

"You must be Kat," she said, her voice weathered like the worn side of a boat, beaten by the sea.

"Friend of Mitch's?" Kat asked.

"He's taken a few of my boats out for some diving expeditions. Has one out now, in fact. Didn't think he'd be out this long."

"That's why we're here," Kat said, gesturing to her girlfriend. "This is Jules. We hadn't heard from him, and I was worried. We thought we might come check the place out and give him a surprise visit if we could find him."

"I'm Pauline." She shook Kat's hand, and Kat noticed the roughness of the woman's palm, worn from ropes wet with sea water. "It's really nice to meet you two. Mitch talks about you a lot. How he wished he get you back out on the water. It looks like maybe he'll get that wish."

"We'll see about that," Kat said, nervously. "You said he had a boat of yours out. Any idea where he went?"

"When he booked the boat, he mentioned a new cave system he'd found. Something deep, something blue, something teeming with life. I've never seen his eyes sparkle like that before. He put together a small team of divers, took his photography gear and deep diving equipment, and set out north. He sent me the coordinates, logged it as a multi-day expedition. That was about four days ago. He should have checked in this afternoon, but I haven't heard anything."

"Do you think we could rent a boat from you? Check those coordinates Mitch left?"

Pauline sighed. "I'll do you one better. I'll go with you. Dammit if that kid isn't one of my best customers. And sweetest. And hey, if this place is half as amazing as he made it sound, I'd love to see it with my own old eyes. I'll die by the water, but I don't know how much sea I have left at this age and with this arthritis kicking in."

Kat softened her posture, grateful for Pauline's offer.

"Thank you. Thank you so much. We can meet you at the dock tomorrow?"

"Seven a.m. sharp. Will be a couple hours out, I think. Pack some food. Bring your own diving gear. Ask for Gil at the shop at the docks. He owes me favor, so tell him I sent you and he'll hook you up with what you need."

"I don't know how I can express just how appreciative I am for this," Kat said, feeling overwhelmed by Pauline's gratitude.

"Just remember this once we're out on the water. Probably the nicest thing I'll ever do for you once we've got the ocean under our feet. She can be cruel when you most need her to be gentle. And I've been known to floor it through the choppiness. Bring your sea legs." Pauline scooted forward, looking at Jules. "And maybe a barf bag or two."

Pauline winked at the girls, a crooked smile on her face. She threw back the rest of her beer in three big mouthfuls.

"See you girls tomorrow morning. Get some good rest tonight. I'll go start getting the boat prepared."

Kat nodded in her direction eagerly, forcing a smile on her face.

## Part Two. Awakening

"Tomorrow," she said.

Pauline moved swiftly out the door, her age belying her confident stride.

Kat turned to Jules.

"You sure you're okay with this? It's a long trip and I know you haven't been on the water as much as I have."

"Are you kidding? I've always wanted to take a boat into the ocean."

"You won't be able to dive though. They won't rent the gear to you if you aren't certified."

Jules looked sheepishly into her pint glass.

"You aren't certified, right?" Kat asked.

"I may have gone through the process a little while back. I was secretly hoping someday I could get you out in the ocean again. I figured that would take one more speedbump out of the process."

"Jules, you're..." Kat's eyes softened. "You're really something. I love you."

"Let's head to the docks and get the gear sorted out. One

less thing to do at the butt crack of dawn tomorrow."

The two stepped down from their stools and headed toward the exit, hand-in-hand.

# Part Three.
# Destabilize

The sun had set by the time Kat and Jules, hand in hand once again, had reached the docks. The dockside storefronts were taking in the last of their customers, turning in their gear for the night, stacking kayaks and paddleboards, water dripping from them after a hose down to remove the sand from their surfaces.

Kat and Jules pushed open the thin wood door to Gil's Gills. The diving shop Pauline had recommended to them was filled with piles of equipment, stacked from floor to ceiling.

"Hello?" Kat called out, unable to see any signs of life amongst the stacks of gear.

A rustling from the back resounded and a wiry man with thick glasses emerged from a backroom.

"Kat and Jules? Pauline called over. Said you were here for some diving gear. I would have just taken some stuff over to her boat, but I wanted to make sure you were sized right and whatnot."

Gil's voice was strained, as if he was trying to put on a cheery front through a troubled disposition. Kat noted that he walked with a slight limp that smoothed out the closer he got to them, as if he eased into his gait.

Kat gave him a gentle smile.

"Thank you so much. Do you have any idea about the coordinates Mitch went to for diving? Any special equipment he needed for his expedition?" Kat asked.

Gil's face contorted into thought. He put his hand behind his head, rubbing his bald patch.

"Nothing out of the ordinary as far as gear went. I don't think he was expecting any trouble. I sure hope he's okay. That boy helps keep this business afloat with all the people he takes out on the water. And he's a real respectable kid too."

Kat smiled warmly. "He's a good brother." Jules squeezed her hand.

"But the coordinates?" Jules asked.

Gil kept quiet, his hand dropping from his head as he

turned to a rack of gear and began rifling through it.

Kat could sense his discomfort. She walked forward and placed a hand on his shoulder, unsure if touching this stranger was the right approach, but she didn't know how else to break the silence.

"Where did he go, Gil?"

Gil relaxed under her touch, letting out a breath that shuddered through old lungs.

"Haven't thought about that place in years, despite the trouble it caused," Gil said after another moment of silence. "I just barely got out."

Kat's heart felt like it jumped off a cliff, wondering what kind of place her brother had adventured to.

Gil continued. His face was slack, his eyes glazed as if he was drifting to some faraway place. "If I'd have known that's where Mitch was headed, I would have sent him packing and done my best to banish him from this island. Didn't know until Pauline sent over the coordinates. Never told anybody about what happened there, even when they asked where the rest of me went."

"Rest of you?" Jules asked.

Gil took of his shoe, revealing a prosthetic underneath. He tapped the limb against the metal rack next to him, a clanking ringing out in the shop.

"Just told everyone it was a shark, and it was taken care of. I shouldn't have been there anyway, but I was lot more adventurous those days. Looking for trouble that I didn't need to find."

Kat's heart was racing, wondering if Mitch had already met his fate. She wondered if they'd find him missing a limb, or if they'd even find him at all.

"Does it have a name?" Kat asked.

"The place or the thing that took my leg?" Gil paused, taking a seat in a chair, holding his head in his hands, staring a hole into the ground. "The place has no name. Just a cave system a ways out. Not many folks have reason to go out that direction. The locals know to stay away, and I try to keep the more exploratory minded from heading out there. Can't always catch them when they lie though."

Kat's blood warmed for a minute at Gil's implication that Mitch was a liar. She felt her temperature rise until she realized that, well, maybe he was a liar, and maybe he had lied in a way that got himself and others into serious trouble.

Gil's deep voice interrupted her thoughts. "The place has no name. And the thing that took my leg? Well, I don't exactly know how to name something when you don't know what it is. I don't remember a body or fins or eyes. All I remember is sharp and pain and hauling ass through the water and back to my boat. I thank whatever being is out there for the tiny shred of luck I must have used in that moment."

Questions swam in Kat's mind that she wasn't sure how to ask. Jules' face was pinched, and Kat could tell she had a few things to say too. But they remained quiet, hoping Gil might fill the void.

"That's all I've got for you. I'm sorry. The ocean is steeped with legends and this island's had her fair share. I only know what happened to me out near where your brother went off to. And I can only hope that whatever got me is dead and gone by now. It's been quiet out there for a while, and I've often wondered if someone finally put it to rest for good. If that's the case, best hope nothing woke it up again."

The girls uttered soft thank yous, unsure of what else to say to Gil. He looked guilty, and Kat wondered if he felt like he was sending them off to their own certain misfortunes.

"I hope you find him," Gil said. "And I hope I get to see your smiling faces when you return my gear. You've got that same look on your face as your brother. Determined, unswayable. I can tell you're going to go after him no matter what I say or do. So please, please just be careful." Gil smiled and chuckled. "And don't let Pauline steamroll the two of you. She's a bit brusque, but she's got a heart that rivals her skill at the captain's wheel."

In silence, the two were fitted for suits by Gil, who loaded a couple of gear bags with the various suits and tools they'd need for the trip.

"I'll have these sent over to Pauline. No need for you two

## Part Three. Destabilize

to trek all that way. I'm sure Pauline told y'all to get a good night's sleep, but I'll echo that. Water's supposed to be rough tomorrow. We'll see what the morning holds."

The girls thanked Gil and headed out the door. The night sky was dim, a bit clouded. The air felt heavy.

As the pair walked back to the hotel, their hands found each other once again. Kat noticed Jules fidgeting with her pocket.

"What do you have there?" Kat asked, curiosity getting the best of her.

Jules blushed. "Nothing, I—"

"Girlies, hey, girlies!" a gravely voice called out to them.

The pair turned towards the boats bobbing by the docks, a flicker of a fire in a barrel caught their eye. An old man warmed his hands over the fire. He locked eyes with Kat, and she felt him digging into her soul.

Kat and Jules attempted to keep walking, trying not to engage.

"Girlies!" He tried again to call them over, whistling

after his shout. "Your brother had a smile just like yours."

That stopped Kat cold in her tracks.

The man continued, having caught her attention. "I say 'had', because he's probably been swallowed up by now." That sent Kat in a beeline towards the man, Jules jogging to keep up.

"What do you know about Mitch?" Kat said through gritted teeth.

"I know that he was eager to die." Kat fought the urge to punch the man who was so clearly toying with her emotions and knew what happened to Mitch. The man held out his hand. "Information ain't cheap, girly."

Jules took out a few bills from her pocket, eager to keep the man talking.

"I told him I could see his soul was looking for adventure. A fight. Something to churn up the waters of his routine. That there were treasures to be found. History to be made. We traded: treasure for treasure." The man nodded to his rucksack next to the barrel of fire. A curled piece of paper stuck out.

## Part Three. Destabilize

Jules knelt down and pulled it from the bag and handed it to Kat. As soon as Kat held it in her hands, felt its weight and gloss, she knew what she'd see when she uncurled the paper.

She held the thick paper in her hands, steeling herself for the barrage of memories that were already fighting to breach the surface. She could almost smell the scent of her mother's hair, clean after a day of diving. Her hair free of the ocean's saliva, the salt washed away down the drain of the shower. Released from the ocean's claim until she'd dive again.

She took a deep breath, and with trembling hands unraveled the paper like she would any other memory—slowly, cautiously, afraid to feel the throes of a heart and mind trapped in the past.

Inch by inch, the old man and Jules drifted away as the image filtered into eyes that had aged considerably since she'd last held this photo.

And there it was. One of her mom's last photographs, taken before the accident. A picture of a dark underwater cave mouth, lit by glowing creatures. Her brother's favorite of their mom's work. Her mother had told them how she loved the way that nature was inviting you to look into the darkness of her depths. Provided her own glowsticks for the journey. Told them you just needed to bring your bravery.

Kat remembered Mitch, teenage legs tucked underneath him, eyes wide like he was a third of his age and seeing the ocean for the first time. He held the picture delicately in his hands while Mom pointed out the different sea creatures she had trapped within her frame. As she rattled off names and rarity and secret little tricks the animals hid away, Mitch's mouth just opened wider and wider until suddenly, it snapped shut as he was shaken from his wondrous thoughts.

"But what's in there?" he asked her, pointing to the dark cave entrance.

"A portal to another dimension," Kat had teased.

Mom laughed, shaking her head. "You're not entirely wrong," she said. And with that, she had Mitch and Kat back on the edge of their seats. "I was able to get in, just a short ways. Reached my camera through a tight hole that I couldn't shimmy

## Part Three. Destabilize

my way into, and clicked."

"And what did you find?" Mitch asked.

A frown crept across her face. "Emptiness." Kat gestured to move her along. "Just emptiness. Darkness. A whole world that I swear should have existed but pretended not to exist."

She started waving her fingers around, tantalizing the teens with the mystery. "I looked at that photo, searched it far and wide for some sign of life. Trying to understand why all I saw was pitch black and the filtered grains of sand."

"Well...?"

"Well," their mom said dramatically, "The only thing I learned that day...was that when you try to photograph something that doesn't want to be seen..."

"C'mon, Mom!" Mitch loudly squeaked out, his pubescent voice cracking.

"...you better not forget the flash."

Kat nearly groaned out loud, remembering the ending to the story. A good memory of her mom. A good last memory.

Mitch must have wanted something badly to give that

away.

Kat narrowed her eyes at the man who had received a treasure he never should have held. "What did you trade him?" she asked, through teeth clenched in anger.

"I traded him a story. I'll trade you too, you give me something you hold dear."

"I don't...I don't have anything," Kat said, trying to hide her bracelet clad wrist behind her back.

Jules stepped forward. "We have more money."

The man shook his head. "Money only gets you this far."

Jules grumbled next to Kat, unsure of how to proceed. Once again, Jules fumbled with her pocket, and Kat wondered what it held. There was a part of her that knew what it probably was, and that part of her knew she needed to keep Jules from giving it up to this disheveled man.

Heart heavy, Kat fondled the gold-colored bracelet on her wrist. "Mitch and I picked these out when we were kids. Joked it was the lifeline between us. Will this work?"

The man pondered her offering, savoring her emotions

## Part Three. Destabilize

radiating off her skin by the glow of the moon. His eyes gleamed. "That'll do."

He gestured to the two to take a seat on a couple of rocks next to the barrel.

"We'll stand," Jules said, arms crossed.

"Suit yourself." The man took a deep breath. "Your brother wasn't looking to discover just anything. Not gold, not a buried shipwreck. He was looking for a legend.

"There's a curse in the sea. He wanted to find it. A man seeking a curse is a dead man and I told him as much, but he wanted to find proof of the legend. Become a legend himself. He'd heard whispers of the thing in the sea that lives near a remote set of caves. He wanted to be the one to photograph it."

Kat ran her hands through her hair. That sounded like him. After their parents died, he wanted so badly to be the son they would be proud of. They were dream chasers, and he was too.

"What is it?" Kat asked. "What is the thing he was looking for?"

"He hadn't a clue really. I didn't tell him. I got the feeling he didn't care what it was—alive, dead, treasure…nothing. I knew he was gonna end up at the bottom of the sea no matter what, so I figured I'd leave him a little bit of excitement. You know those games where you put your hand into a box covered in a black cloth and try to guess what you're touching? The real game isn't about getting it right. The real game is about gathering the nerves to stick your vulnerable fingers into the unknown when everyone but you can see what's on the other side." He cleared his throat, dislodged a glob of spit and phlegm from his sinuses and spat it onto the ground next to him.

"I knew that boy would stick his hand in any box, no matter the shape or size or danger within. So, I helped him explore. He was sad to pass over that photo, but his face lit up with a fire like the stars when I told him where to go. See? I'm not so bad." He laughed, a rattling thing that clawed its way up from his chest.

Kat was losing her temper, but she didn't want to act rashly and have the stranger clam up on her. She could tell Jules

## Part Three. Destabilize

was feeling angered too, could feel her hand tightening her hold on her own, her nails digging trenches into her skin.

"But you?" The old man grinned, his teeth rotted, whistling through gaps in his gums. "I'll tell you what to expect. You're not looking to find it, but I want you to have a fighting chance when it finds you.

"What lives at the bottom of the ocean, what tore its way through this coast a century ago before resting under the covers of the sandy sheets of the sea?" He paused, his hand rising to his face, gnarled into a point that ended in the direction of his mouth. "It's teeth, plain and simple. A creature—if you can call it that—damned to hunt. No body, just *it*, nothing more than a swirl of teeth and debris gathered from the ocean floor, spinning like a saw blade."

The visuals in Kat's mind were nothing short of horrifying, trying to imagine what a vortex of teeth could look like—and what it could do. Her mind began to buzz like the chainsaw the man described. A horrible whining, muffled sound lost to the folds of her brain, snuffed out by the waves of the sea.

The stranger continued his tale, delighting in the perturbed look on Kat's face. "It was created from nothing. A bastard of the waves. Brought to us by a wizened woman filled with grief."

Despite the frustration and anger at the man's apparent role in Mitch's death, Kat was engrossed in the tale. "How?" she asked.

"A woman who lived on this coast a century ago created the bodiless monster. Filled with rage and despair, she threw a marble into the sea—her son's favorite toy. Something so simple, so mundane. Something we all do today, throwing things into the water to see what becomes of it, to never see it again. A message in a bottle. An empty bottle of beer." The man took a swig of his own amber drink. Then another.

Kat thought back to all the shells she'd thrown back to the ocean as a child, wanting to return then to the water where they belonged. Cringing, she recalled when she had dumped the contents of a garbage can off the side of a boat in a moment of childish curiosity. Her Dad had scolded her firmly and sent her

## Part Three. Destabilize

and Mitch to the water to clean up their messes. Looking back, she regretted what fell to the bottom of the ocean. The sea could take, but she also wished humans wouldn't give it what it doesn't deserve.

Wiping his lips, the stranger continued his tale. "Her son had played in the sand with a set of marbles for hours by the ocean while she scrubbed barnacles off of ships. Alone, he'd toss the marbles back and forth, practicing his aim, concocting rules for games he'd only ever play against his shadow. She could keep an eye on him, from the corner of her vision in between the endless labor of scrubbing ships. But even if she had only looked away for a moment, the ocean would have capitalized on her mistake."

Kat and Jules shared a glance, knowing where this story was going but unable to stop the stranger's words from entering their ears and settling into the darkest places of their minds.

"In an overzealous toss, the boy threw a marble into the pile already collected into a pocket of sand. With all his might, he propelled the finicky glass, which bounced off of the sedentary marbles and into the tumbling waves of the tide. He lost it in the froth, running after it into the ocean where he'd been instructed to never breach as he couldn't swim. It didn't take long for the hands of the ocean to steal him for herself."

Kat shuddered, imagining how horrifying it would be to see your son, then nothing, in the blink of an eye. Her heart ached for the nameless mother.

"The woman took to the water, but it was too late. His body never returned to the shore. She was left with nothing but the remnants of the unknowable games he'd played with his collection of marbles. She scooped up the trinkets, cradling them in her hands before the sea could take those, too."

Kat saw Jules wipe a tear from her eye, always the one to be freer with her emotions. Kat wondered then if she was harming her partner, her love, by having her here.

The man gave Kat a knowing look, taking one last long swig of his beer before finishing his tale.

"A week later, the woman returned to the last place she'd seen her son. Though little time had passed, it felt like a lifetime.

## Part Three. Destabilize

And she'd spent that lifetime with a marble in her hands. Rubbing its surface over and over with each memory of her son, salted with her grief, she smoothed the marble into a more perfect version of itself. Cleaned of sand, but heavy with despair, she threw that marble to her son. With a soft plunk in ever-churned water, the marble sank to its own grave. She gave the marble to the sea, screaming curses. She rattled its bones, and they came loose. A vortex emerged. A whirlpool gathered discarded teeth and refuse from the ocean floor. Fueled by her anger, it spins in infinite destruction. Taking what's lost, giving it a home, destroying the unknown."

"What happened to the woman?" Kat asked.

"The ocean whispers of her death. Said that she leapt to the middle of the teeth, shredded herself down to the bone through the center of the spinning sharp circle. The loss of her son had already stripped her of her heart, so the sea took the rest."

Kat shook her head. "So, you didn't tell Mitch any of this? What if he meets this monster?"

The old man barked a laugh. "My guess is that he already has."

Jules gripped Kat's hand tightly again. "He probably just ran out of gas out there. Great story and all, super happy ending. But there's no way that's true."

Kat still felt the emptiness of her brother's link in her gut. She wanted to doubt the tall tale, but she couldn't risk being wrong and unprepared.

"Wait, where did you tell him to go?"

The old man shook his head back and forth, wispy white hair shining in the moonlight. "I gave you enough information."

"C'mon, Kat," Jules said. "We already know where we're going."

Kat knew that was the truth, but she wanted to know what he told Mitch. What his ears had heard. Maybe it would make her feel closer to him.

"It's all bullshit anyway," Jules said, urging her away from the man. "A waste of a perfectly good bracelet." She wished Jules would stop playing whatever card she thought she

## Part Three. Destabilize

had. It was a farfetched story, but Kat had that feeling swirling in her gut that told her not to disregard the man's words. She was turning it over in her mind, power-washing the details to see what nuggets of truth were left behind.

"Can it be killed?" Kat asked the man.

"Not by harpoon or gun. No body to destroy. But the marble is its core. It lays exposed to the ring of teeth, surrounded by death. It seeks shelter."

Kat contemplated the old man's words.

Silence hung in the air until Jules broke it, tugging on Kat's arm to head back to the hotel. "Well, provided that you aren't full of complete and utter shit, thank you for the information."

The man smiled, his rotten teeth flashing again. "The sea thanks you for your offering. Good luck out there, girlies."

The couple walked away, new mysteries of the water filling their heads. Kat didn't know whether to believe the old man, but she knew in her heart she'd find her answers in the morning. His story fueled the smoldering of the memories she kept pushing down. Of teeth snapping. Of missing friends and family. Of something in the crystal sea that couldn't be killed or even found unless it wanted you to.

Blood-filled water coated the back of Kat's eyelids as she drifted to sleep, dreaming of tides and death.

# Part Four.
# Churn

A little past seven in the morning, the boat pulled away from the docks and headed towards the last coordinates that Mitch had logged. With Pauline at the wheel, Kat and Jules huddled close on the boat.

It had been a long night. Restless. Dreams and worries rippling through waking moments. Despite the cool air, Kat had sweated through her thin layer of clothes at the whim of her anxieties. It wasn't until Jules had glued herself to Kat's back, despite the wet material clinging to her skin, that the two had finally fallen asleep. Cradled, settled, together.

Now, with the shore behind them, the wind whipped around their heads, their ponytailed hair slapped their backs, and there was only forward to go.

Kat looked at the sky, pink swirling with the clouds on the horizons.

"Red sky in the morning, sailors take warning," Kat

muttered under her breath.

"A little storm would make this just the perfect outing," Jules said, her arm around Kat's shoulder.

On cue, the sky opened up and started to drizzle.

Kat thought Jules looked beautiful out on the ocean. She wished she had gone out on the water in circumstances other than this, a frenzied attempt to find a twin she was becoming more and more convinced was gone. She knew that she had done right by Jules over their several years together, but it didn't stop her from wishing she had done better.

The engine was steady, loud and powerful as it fought the waves, heading closer to the destination. Pauline had said few words while they packed the boat earlier, her eyes squinting into the distance as if she knew they'd meet some unknowable end. Before disembarking, she'd given the couple a short tour of the boat, modest in its size and worn from use. All that mattered to Kat was that it took her to answers.

There was still at least an hour left of their journey. The boat chugged along, the GPS indicating that things were gliding along undisturbed.

The couple stood up and checked in with Pauline.

"Everything okay up here?" Jules asked.

"Right as rain," Pauline replied, gesturing to the droplets gathering on the boat's surface.

"Anything we can do to help?"

"Just don't puke on my boat."

Kat watched the woman at the wheel, feeling confident in her experienced hands. She looked at home on the water. Pauline's eyes were narrowed as they winced into the sun, partially shielded by dark clouds.

Her prowess at the helm of the boat reminded Kat of the easy confidence her parents exuded. Diving and photography, navigation and technical equipment had always seemed like such a nightmare to Kat's inexperienced eyes. She always wanted to be able to be as knowledgeable and skillful as her parents, wanted to understand the ins and outs of something and be good at it. Looking at Jules, she realized she had succeeded at that at least once in her life.

"You look miles away," Pauline said, taking a moment to acknowledge her company.

"Just wondering what we'll find when we get there, is all," Kat said.

Jules squeezed her hand before turning to Pauline. "Have you heard of the Teeth?"

Pauline scoffed. "Just more tales from the sea. She's filled with legends, few of them real. The only true legends are the seafarers who challenged her waves and won."

"Mitch seemed to believe it," Kat said.

"If he believed that whisper of a tale, he's not the intelligent boy I thought he was."

"That old man seemed to believe it too."

"That old bah humbag-of-bones out by the docks? He'll tell you any story for a couple of bucks."

Jules laughed. "It did seem kind of fake. Throw a marble into the sea and make a teeth demon?"

Pauline smirked. "People are always throwing things into the ocean. Adding pages to her story. Ashes of the dead,

## Part Four. Churn

cannonballs in the middle of wars. Skipping stones on her surface." Pauline moved a stray wisp of hair from her face. "If something bad happened with every item that gets tossed into the ocean, there'd be no way to swim in her depths."

Kat hoped Pauline was right. The rain picked up its intensity, mirroring the storm inside Kat's head.

"Hold on out there," Pauline said from the wheel. "Choppy waters ahead."

Pauline handled the boat, keeping it from jerking about too harshly as the waves grew higher. Long, tense minutes passed as Kat nervously chewed her lip, waiting for the rough patch to be in the rearview.

When the water calmed—at least for the moment—Pauline spoke up again.

"You want to know what I think happened? It isn't pretty, but more likely than the damn Teeth."

Kat pulled her jacket tighter around her shoulders, wary of what the sea-hardened woman might say.

Pauline gestured to the sky and water around them.

"Conditions like this? Boat mighta capsized."

As awfully simple and tragic as it was, it seemed reasonable enough to Kat. Except for that nagging in her stomach.

Pauline continued. "And if that's not enough, some animal *has* been striking the area for the past few days. Just yesterday, after you two left the bar, I saw a report of some remains that washed up on the shore just a town away. In this direction, too."

Kat's stomach sank. She felt like a fool for believing a tall tale when there was enough viciousness in the water to take a life without supernatural cause.

"Every ten years or so, it just kinda happens, you know?" Pauline shrugged. "Someone takes a boat where they shouldn't be going—not unlike what we're doing now, mind you—and bad things happen. Bad, *natural*, things. In fact, bodies, pieces of bodies, even, washing up on shore are just part of the cycle. You fuck with the wrong thing, and even when you're surrounded by water, you're going to get burned."

Silence hung over the women. Kat wondered if Pauline was right, or if maybe the Teeth were responsible for it all. Why couldn't that be a possibility too?

Pauline continued, belaboring the point. Kat wondered if at this point she was still trying to convince them or convince herself.

"You met Gil, right? Lost his leg because he got too drunk and stupid one day to save his own skin. Tried to go diving where the sun don't shine and forgot the simplest rule about the ocean."

"What's that?" Jules asked.

"That shit lives in it. And that shit gets hungry."

Kat could hardly believe Pauline's cavalier attitude about her friend's lost limb, but opted to not say something and anger their captain.

Jules' eyes met Kat's, heavy with worry. "Accidents happen, right?" Jules said. "Sometimes it's a shark. Sometimes it could be some legend come to life." Pauline snorted. "And sometimes, it's just boat trouble and people get saved," Jules said, her eyes on Kat, trying to send her soothing messages.

"Sure, but don't let her lull you into a false sense of security," Pauline said, pointing to the water. "You just wait. As soon as you feel like the storm's over and things are fine, the real trouble begins."

As if controlled by the older woman's whims, the rain started back up again, more relentless than before. The boat bobbed and struggled against the waves for what felt like an eternity, water splashing onto the floor at Kat and Jules' feet. As the hour dredged on, Kat felt the pressure in her chest building, the hollowness of her core pressing outwards against her sides. Memories of her brother crushing her beneath his body surfaced again, making it hard to breathe. She could feel the panic setting in.

Kat and Jules held each other close as they neared the coordinates.

A shape emerged on the waterline past the crest of the waves slamming into the boat. Kat couldn't see into the water—too muddled by frothy surges—but she knew as they approached the shadow that the answers lay underneath.

"We're coming up on the boat!" Pauline shouted.

Kat watched through the raindrops falling from the sky into open water as the boat came into view. The boat was eerily still, bobbing up and down, no movement within. No people appeared, no arms waving the approaching ship down. No head of shaggy blonde hair or matching gold bracelet glinting in what sliver of sun there was. What little hope had bolstered her heart bottomed out as her stomach dropped.

The boat idled up to the seemingly abandoned vessel, anchored to the sea floor. A light flickered within the other boat's bowels.

"Might be someone below. Maybe taking shelter from the rain," Jules said.

"I'll go check," Pauline offered. "Little hard to get across in this weather." She secured a life jacket to her body.

"How the hell is she planning on getting across?" Jules asked.

"I hope to God she isn't trying to just jump it."

The two boats were side by side, jerking about on the waves. Pauline steadied herself on the edge of the boat.

Kat started towards Pauline, hand out trying to stop Pauline from making the leap.

"Hey, Pauline don't—"

But she'd already jumped. Seconds passed like minutes as Pauline hung in the air. For the barest of moments it looked like there was no way Pauline would cross the distance. Kat's heart hammered in her chest as Pauline's arms pinwheeled, attempting to keep her balance in the chasm between the boats.

Her feet thunked against the floor of the other boat. Kat let out the breath she was holding.

"I'm heading down!" Pauline shouted, her hands cupped around her mouth, amplifying her voice through the howling wind.

Pauline disappeared into the ship. Kat and Jules stared across the sea and eagerly awaited her return. Kat wondered if there was anything below, knowing it was naive to think her brother would just be hanging out inside the boat.

## Part Four. Churn

"Do you hear that?" Kat asked, as a gentle humming began, nestled in the sounds of the storm.

"What?"

"A humming. Like a singsong voice of a woman."

Jules strained her ears, trying to hear what Kat described, finding nothing but the noises of water splatting to the deck of the boat and the howl of the wind. She shook her head.

Kat followed the sound, leaning over the edge of the railing, ears perked towards the water below. It was still there, growing louder as if it was coming closer.

Before she could locate the lonely song dripping from the sea, a gray head of hair reemerged from the other boat's belly. Pauline's face surfaced, white as a sheet. Her hands were red with blood. The wind picked up momentum, beating against the women. Rain struck their faces, large droplets obscuring their vision.

Pauline shouted something from across the divide, but the words were jumbled against the backdrop of the storm. She held her arms up, gnarling her hands.

"His ha…miss…dead," was all the pair could hear. The song clapped louder as the waves grew more violent, rocking the boats. That word "dead" made its way through Kat's muddled mind, ringing a bell of clarity that caused a shot of anxiety to spike through her chest. But then, that song. Louder, so mournful, and amplified by the waves of the ocean. Kat was mesmerized by the sound, but resisted the urge to dive into the water and be cradled by the forlorn humming.

Pauline moved closer to the side of the ship, screaming at the girls again, her words inaudible as a roll of thunder swept them away. Jules tried to lean in to catch her speech. Kat leaned in towards the whimsical sobbing of the ocean's song.

Whatever Pauline was saying was cut off as a massive wave attacked the side of the boat.

If it was only the wave, Pauline may have been knocked back into the boat, or at worst, overboard into the chop below.

If it was only a wave, the girls may have been able to salvage their new friend from the water, a little worse for the wear.

## Part Four. Churn

It wasn't only a wave that hit her.

It was a wave, and a circle of teeth.

# Part Five.
# Swallow

The Teeth rode the crest, spinning infinitely like a gnashing hoop of death. The wave overtook Pauline, her body entering one side. She emerged from the other side a shell of a human, shredded as if she'd gone through a woodchipper, bits of bones and flesh flying through the air.

Jules turned to her side and threw up.

Kat stared in disbelief. The legend was real.

The Teeth were hungry.

"Jesus!" Jules yelled, wiping her mouth. "Was that it?"

Kat nodded, her stomach sloshing about like the violent water below. She couldn't believe how fast that thing had torn Pauline apart. She caught the triangles of teeth from the mouths of a thousand sharks spinning. No body, just blades of bone.

And the whole time the wave had devoured the older woman, it had hummed, the same delicate tune that Kat couldn't shake, could barely hear above it. It was louder, all around, expansive and mournful and folding onto itself.

A wave struck the boat again, the Teeth chewing the wood paneling and the fiberglass structure. Another wave slapped the back of the boat, the engine torn to pieces, metal fragments flying out the back of the churning water.

The couple didn't know what to do, at a loss for how to stop the monstrous spinning water devil. They couldn't go *into* the water. The boat was bound to break to pieces soon. They couldn't stay here either.

Jules ran to the control center of the boat, held a speaker and mic to her mouth and ear, attempting to signal help. She knew it would never get there in time, but maybe if she could just let someone know that this monster was *real* and *hungry* they'd have a better chance. And maybe, just maybe they'd get something there that moved faster—a chopper or speedboat.

The static of the radio taunted the pair, broken up by what sounded like attempts of a receiving party to reply. Words were garbled, offering no reassurance that their pleas were heard, let alone a slice of solace for the couple to cling to. Her

## Part Five. Swallow

cries for help were cut off when the boat began to tip. The handhelds flew from Jules' grasp, their thick plastic careening into the console. Kat ran into the enclave, and the couple clasped hands, closed tightly around one another.

"You okay?" Jules asked.

Kat nodded, her face white.

"We have to get to the other boat! It might buy us a little time," Kat said, her voice shaking at the prospect of leaping across the dark chasm. The waves were crashing against the sides of the boats, making the jump more daunting than before.

Kat hated even suggesting it, seeing how fast that wave of the Teeth overtook Pauline, but the boat they were on was nearly thrashed and ready to sink. The other boat seemed to be made of something that the Teeth had more difficulty tearing apart and digesting. Was that even the word for what it had done? Kat's stomach roiled again in rebellion at what Pauline had become. Obliterated. Chunks. Shards of bone that for all she knew joined the circle of Teeth in their chaos.

Jules looked equally conflicted, but knew what her

partner had suggested was quickly becoming their only option.

"Go!" Jules yelled.

Another wave hit, mingled with the Teeth, tearing more fiberglass from the frame and sending the boat careening back and forth.

"Now!"

As one side of the boat tipped towards the gray sky, reaching new heights as it sank, the girls scrabbled over to the railing. Jules climbed faster to the side, reaching the top and hurling herself to the other boat.

Kat felt her stomach lurch again at the prospect of the jump. But there was Jules, safely on the other side, encouraging her.

She climbed. One foot after another. As she prepared herself, bending her legs, the humming and whirring of the Teeth mounted, like someone had grabbed the volume dial of the water and cranked it for all it was worth. It sent Kat off balance just enough to slow her momentum as she leapt.

She wished she had landed as gracefully as Jules.

## Part Five. Swallow

Instead, her upper torso just barely cleared the other boat's railing, sending a shock of pain shooting into her midsection. The air rushed from her body as she was once again reminded of her worst childhood memory of the cruelest version of her brother. *Crushed sides, crushed sides, can't breathe, drowning.* Finally, lyrics to accompany the ferocious crooning of the Teeth's humming.

Kat wheezed, her lungs burning. Jules scrabbled to her partner, grabbing her slick hands.

"I've got you, baby. I've got you, I swear," Jules chanted as she attempted to pull her partner over the side and to relative safety. And she did, so close, so close, *so close* to making it before the Teeth returned.

As Kat's body tumbled over the railing and into the boat, water bit at her heels. In a sobbing hum, the Teeth attacked and her foot got caught in the tip of the wave. When she hit the other side, she screamed at her stump of a foot.

Blood pumped steadily from the severed portion of her leg. Kat moaned in pain.

"Oh god, oh godgodgod," Jules mumbled, watching her partner roll on the deck in agony. Kat made terrible noises, and her leg was devoid of her foot. It took everything Jules had to keep from passing out.

"Fuuuuck!" Kat moaned, drawing out the lone vowel for a few seconds before biting her lip.

Jules ripped her jacket from around her shoulders, the material already saturated by the torrential downpour.

"I'm sorry, so sorry," she whispered as she cinched the material tightly in an attempt to staunch the flow of blood.

Outside the ship, the Teeth loomed, circling around and around. The women couldn't see it move, couldn't see it froth the water in its anguish. But above her own groans of pain and Jules' steady apologies, Kat could hear the humming traveling the circumference of their position. Louder, left, across, right, louder again the sorrowful song danced around her, taunting her.

Before she knew it, Jules had wrapped her arms under her shoulders. "Hold your leg up so it doesn't drag," she instructed. Kat obeyed, wrapping her white-knuckled hand

## Part Five. Swallow

around her knee and lifting, not daring to stare at the bloody stump.

"I'm going to take you down below, okay?" Jules told her, not waiting for her permission to start tugging. "I love you, Kat. I love you," she said between hefts.

It was too much movement for Kat's pain-riddled body. Her ribs complained the whole way, threatening to turn themselves into shards and pierce everything she was inside. Every jiggle of her injured leg sent jolts of agony throughout her body, and she wished she would just pass the fuck out already, but she needed to stay with Jules. So, she pushed and pushed and crab-walked her other leg beneath her, screaming the whole way, her torment joining the anguished wails of the storm and the Teeth's frenzied circular path.

After several minutes of the awkward and agonizing journey, the two women were lying on the floor of the boat's cabin. They were both spent. Jules was grateful they were alive. Kat wanted to be grateful, but was in too much pain to know if she was.

Kat's eyes roamed the room, trying to focus on anything but the pain. Her eyes settled on the blue flooring of the boat in the center of the room. No…not a floor, but a window. A cabin-side view of the ocean below. *God Mitch sure had sprung for a bougie boat*, she thought, waves of delirium clouding her vision. Kat wished the water was so much further away than just a pane of glass.

"God, please just kill my leg," Kat said, settling on gratitude that was somewhere in between.

"I wish I could find an off button for you." Jules leaned her head close to Kat's, trying to take in the fact that her girlfriend was still very much so alive.

"I've never wished I was an action figure more than in this moment. Just pop the leg off and replace it with another."

Jules laughed, whispering "I love you" to Kat before her laughter devolved into sobs. They lay on the floor together, trapped by the vulnerability of their predicament, unsure if they'd ever get out.

After a moment, Jules sat up, and pulled Kat's head into

## Part Five. Swallow

her lap.

Kat looked into her partner's deep brown eyes, searching them for answers to questions she dare not speak.

"What the fuck are we going to do?" Jules asked.

"Know how to drive a boat?"

"I sure as hell can try."

"Controls are topside, I think. Don't want to go back up there. Don't want you to, either."

Jules' face paled as she pointed to the corner of the room. "Well, we have to do something unless we want to end up like him."

Kat craned her neck from her position on the floor, looking at where Jules' concentration was focused.

"Oh," she said, her voice a sharp whisper.

In the corner of the room, a man with dark hair was slumped. Beneath him, a puddle of blood had formed and dried. His gray skin was already beginning to decay in the salty and wet conditions of the ocean. The smell of his decrepit state slammed into them through the briny air, sour and sweet and rotten and so, so much of it all.

It was then that Kat realized what Pauline had been yelling from across the violent water.

"His hands are missing. He's dead."

They were. He was.

Jules was a sour green, trying not to gag.

"Did you know him?"

"No. I didn't really know the people my brother dove with." Regret flooded her body.

"Do you think they got him? The Teeth?"

"Sure looks like it. Wasn't looking to drive a boat with what he had left, I suppose. Looks like he bled out. Fast."

"We won't let that happen to you."

Kat turned her head, trying to settle into Jules' lap. She felt it, then, the hard object in Jules' pocket. The thing she'd been fidgeting with off and on over the course of their trip.

"Jules?" she said softly, glancing at her pocket.

"You know what it is. You know I love you."

And she did.

## Part Five. Swallow

"I do."

In that moment, Kat married Jules in her mind, kissed her hard in their moment of true happiness. But in reality, her strength wavered, and her eyes fluttered, startling Jules into action, no time spared to discuss the wedding they'd never have.

Jules stood up and began to rifle through drawers, grabbing towels.

Kat was feeling fainter as the minutes passed.

As Jules searched for First Aid supplies, Kat watched the blue of the water beneath the boat. She was surprised to see it look so calm, as if there wasn't a storm raging above and a whirlwind of homicidal, grief-fueled teeth hellbent on destruction within the wind and waves.

Just shining sapphire, no doubt teeming with life deep below, taking shelter from the weather, finding peace in the far corners of the sea.

A school of fish, shimmering in the lowlight. Sand, far, far below. A bed of kelp.

Open water.

Quickly filled by gnashing, swirling, blood-stained teeth.

"Oh, fuck!" Kat yelled.

"What? What happened?"

Kat tried to roll away from the glass, making herself invisible to the Teeth, hoping, praying that they didn't catch her trembling form.

"The Teeth! The fucking Teeth." Jules rushed over to Kat's prone form. "No! Don't let it see you."

Jules swallowed loudly.

"Too late."

The Teeth didn't have eyes, but if it did, Kat suspected they'd be narrowed, creases between them, and its mouth would be open in a snarl.

"Dammit, dammit…" Jules trailed off. "Okay, if it's under there, I'm going up."

Kat didn't want Jules to leave, but she knew it had to be done.

"Hurry," she said, brushing Jules' cheek with her lips. "I

love you."

"I love you, too." A quick kiss on the lips, forehead, and then Jules climbed the short set of stairs.

Kat faced the glass floor again. The Teeth hovered, fragments of sharp objects eclipsing the open water, filling it with its threats.

"Fuck you," Kat said.

The humming was loud, growing louder in anger.

And that's when she saw it. The gold of a chain glinted in the water. A twin to the bracelet she'd exchanged for a story. Mitch's bracelet, which once held her Dad's wedding ring.

Her brother was dead. The Teeth had stolen his bracelet. This whole trip and all of its devastation ending in one anticlimactic glimpse of her dead brother's bracelet. She'd never get to punch his shoulder for the trouble he caused. She'd never get to make him groan at her jokes again. She'd never see the rest of him.

She screamed at the ring of death. Kat wished that thing had a face so she could see it cower in fear.

The Teeth shot forward, tinking against the glass.

"Ha, fucking, ha," Kat said, all but cackling at the feeble attempts of the whirring Teeth.

She watched the bracelet, hovering in the center of the serrated objects thrashing back and forth. And next to that…a marble. It was a fucking marble. Just like the old man had described. That marble still looking as new as the day it was held between the fingers of a boy who would die.

Her disbelief was pushed to the side when the Teeth rammed the glass once more. They jolted against the floor again. Again, and again.

Kat's weak laughter bubbled up as the predicament worsened. *How much more could she take?* Her frustrated laughter trailed off as cracks appeared across the transparent material.

"Shit." She rocked herself to a sitting position, eyes darting around the cabin for a crutch. A lifeboat paddle that had been tossed into a corner caught her eye.

The glass beneath her spiderwebbed as the Teeth threw

## Part Five. Swallow

everything it had against the surface. Kat could hear the glass breaking under the pressure as she crawled as fast as she could on her knees to the oar. She bit her lip until it bled as the stump of her leg errantly hit the floor every few yards.

Her fingers gripped the smooth wood of the paddle, her hand wrapping around it like she'd found God and would never let go. Salvation, short-lived as the glass exploded inward and water poured into the cabin, filling the floor with its briny exploration.

Kat screamed again as the saltwater hit her injured leg as she hobbled to the stairs.

"Jules!" she yelled. "Please, Jules!"

Before she could cry out again, her girlfriend's arms pulled her up the stairs, back to the deck of the boat.

The two huffed on the floor, desperation in their eyes.

"Engine's dead," Jules said.

"Doesn't matter. She's filling with water. She's going to sink."

"This sucks."

"Really does."

The two sat in silence, cradling each other in what they believed to be their final moments. The boat groaned as it took on water.

The Teeth returned to the side of the boat, the humming that sounded like a weeping woman intensifying before breaking against the sinking ship.

The boat tipped, tossing the women across the deck.

Jules rushed back to Kat, calling out to her partner, reaching for her from a yard away.

A last-ditch attempt to hold the hand of the one she loved.

A wave, ten feet in height, crested over the top of the boat, taking Jules into the viciously convulsing water. The Teeth ate Jules and spat her remains into Kat's face, the warmth splattering her wind burned cheeks.

Letting out a guttural cry, Kat felt her soul rip in half, gone in an instant. She didn't even have time to feel the myriad of things swirling inside her. No time to think about the years

## Part Five. Swallow

she wouldn't have with Jules. No time to think about how Jules—Goddammit *Jules*—had risked it all for her. She choked on the sob, held it in until it filled her lungs and entered her veins and finally spilled from her lips in something that sounded as inhuman as the Teeth were.

The sea had taken everything from her.

Kat's hands gripped her leg tightly, trying to will the pain away, only moving her hands to wipe the chunks of her lover off of her cheek. The shock and adrenaline confused her body and mind, and her head spun like a whirlpool.

She staggered to a hunched standing position, hopping to the side of the boat trying to find the circle of teeth in the water below. She spotted it, spinning its wheel of death away from the boat, turning back to finish the job.

With nothing left to give except herself, Kat climbed to the side of the boat. Not much time to do anything different. Out of options. The boat was sinking. Her lover was gone. Her brother was dead. The Teeth approached. She had to time it just right, position herself for success with the only plan she had. The gold of Mitch's bracelet glittered in the weak sun. She waited for it to pass, just barely, and then jumped from the edge of the boat.

The salt stung her bleeding wound. The cold water bit deep into her body.

Kat reoriented herself behind the teeth, still on its path to the boat. From her position, she saw it. A tiny, glass marble at the center of the circle.

She swam, kicking her maimed legs with all her might. Her lungs burned, bubbles streaming from her mouth as she reached for the small, round marble at the center of the teeth. She wondered if she'd even have any fingers left to grip the floating orb.

The sharp objects spinning in anger chewed her up as much as it could before it suddenly halted. Kat could only feel the marble in her hand, her body not registering the missing flesh around her torso and arms.

Her hand closed around the glass toy, feeling its vibration in her palm. Pulling the marble to her chest, Kat folded her body around the dense sphere.

Shelter. She held the marble close, feeling its glassy smooth surface nestled between her breasts.

The teeth fell around her, sinking to the ocean floor. The white triangles shifted back and forth as they descended, like coins dropped into a wishing well as they sank.

Kat sank with them, her lungs out of air, her legs out of energy, her heart out of love.

She fell, watching as the teeth blinked in and out, no longer rotating in their deadly design. Bits of flesh and bone fell around her, too. Surrounded by her lover, her chest burned as she cried, tears never standing on their own, absorbed by the ocean deep.

Torn wetsuit pieces, flaps of rubber from fins. The divers the teeth had consumed days before floated down. Kat's vision spotted black, unable to discern the cloth and broken equipment swirling around her from the specks of her life fading, consciousness leaving her.

Her knees hit the bottom, and her body curled into the

sand.

She held the marble tight against her, under her arms, tucked to her chest, and she soaked up the emotion of the sea. Lives lost. Found. Lost again.

Her eyes fluttered, nothing left in her tank.

As she closed her eyes, choking on the water in a final shudder, she caught the glimmer of a gold bracelet and a silver engagement ring, nestling together into the sand near her cheek.

# Epilogue.
# Regurgitate

At the bottom of the ocean, a body decomposed. Skin rotted away, beaten by sand and salt over the years. A marble, smoothed evermore by time, slipped from between bony fingers and fell the short distance to the sand below.

The cycle began again.

The marble screamed to the sea.

Unearthed, the Teeth answered.

END

# About the Author

Nikki R. Leigh is a queer, forever-90s kid wallowing in all things horror. When not writing horror fiction and poetry, she can be found creating custom horror-inspired toys, making comics, and hunting vintage paperbacks. She reads her stories to her partner and her cat, one of which gets scared very easily.

# Also Available from Spooky House Press

*Helicopter Parenting in the Age of Drone Warfare* by Patrick Barb

*The White Horse* by Rebecca Harrison

*Deeply Personal* by Alexis Macaluso

*Boarded Windows, Dead Leaves* by Michael Jess Alexander

*The Disappearance of Tom Nero* by TJ Price

*Her Infernal Name & Other Nightmares* by Robert P. Ottone

*Residents of Honeysuckle Cottage* by Elizabeth Davidson

# Coming Soon

*Clairviolence Vols. 1 & 2* by Mo Moshaty

*Star Shapes* by Ivy Grimes

Made in the USA
Monee, IL
15 December 2024